For Ollie, Alice and Lexie S.P-H.

For Theodore, my little digger expert! E.E.

READY, STEADY, DIG!

First published in 2015 by Hodder Children's Books

Text copyright © Smriti Prasadam-Halls 2015
Illustration copyright © Ed Eaves 2015

Hodder Children's Books
An imprint of Hachette Children's Group
Part of Hodder & Stoughton
Carmelite House, 50 Victoria Embankment
London EC4Y 0DZ

A catalogue record of this book is available from the British Library.

ISBN: 978 1444 92359 9
10 9 8 7 6 5 4 3 2 1

Printed in China

An Hachette UK Company
www.hachette.co.uk

FSC
www.fsc.org

MIX
Paper from
responsible sources
FSC® C104740

h
Hodder
Children's
Books

Ready, Steady, DIG!

Smriti Prasadam-Halls   Ed Eaves

Let's go to work, Construction Crew!
Time to see what you can do.
Put your toughness to the test,
Build, build, build your very best.

Motors starting, **BRMM BRMM BRMM!**
Engines revving, **VRMM VRMM VRMM!**

Get in gear, don't be slow!
Ready, steady... **OFF WE GO!**

CONNOR CRANE is at the ready,
With his steel chain holding steady.

High up hanging,
CLINGING, CLANGING.

His wrecking ball goes BASH, BASH, **BASH!**
Ready, steady...
SMASH, SMASH, **CRASH!**

DUMPER DAVE is big and tough,
For any job, he's strong enough.

CREEPING, CRAWLING,

HEAVING,

HAULING.

Rubble in his sturdy skip. Now, ready, steady...

TIP, TIP, TIP!

MIXER MILLIE spins and hums,
Cement is churning in her drum.

BARREL WHIRLING,
CONCRETE SWIRLING.

Spread it thick to build and fix,
Ready, steady...
MIX, MIX, MIX, MIX!

RAVI ROLLER takes his spot,
Squashing tarmac, wet and hot.

SQUELCHING,

SPLATTERING,

SQUEEZING,

FLATTENING.

Press it smooth, no bumps or holes,
Ready, steady...

ROLL,
ROLL, ROLL!

DOUG THE DIGGER

loves to dig,
Gobbling earth,
however big.

MUNCHING, CRUNCHING,
SCRAPING, SCRUNCHING.

...OOPS!

Oh dear, oh dear, what bad luck,
Doug the Digger's

STUCK, STUCK, STUCK!

He gives a **YELL,**
he gives a **SHOUT,**
Can anybody get him out?

ALL his friends roar into action,
Wheels a-turning, gaining traction.

WELL DONE, TEAM! All safely back!
Now let's keep going, stay on track.
Complete the project, brick by brick,
And get the job done,
DOUBLE QUICK.

Shunting, shifting,
loading, lifting,

Using all your strength and skill.
READY, STEADY...

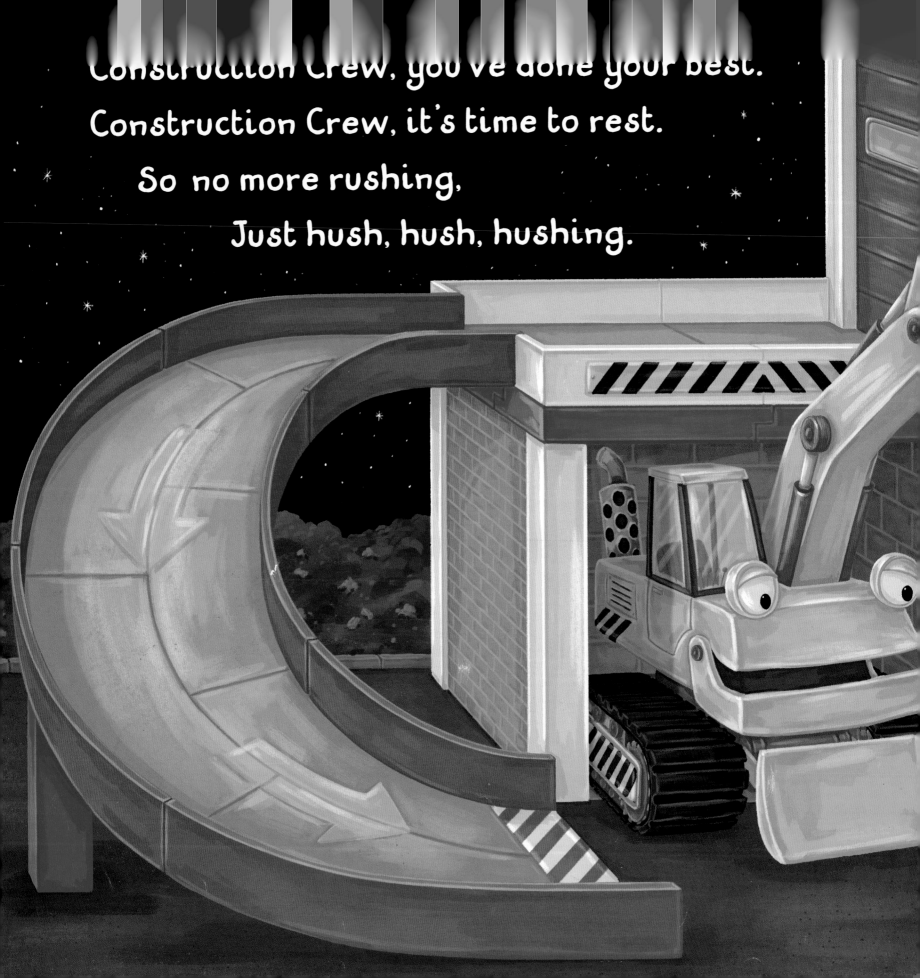

Construction Crew, you've done your best.
Construction Crew, it's time to rest.
So no more rushing,
Just hush, hush, hushing.

Not another HONK or BEEP...

READY, STEADY...
time to SLEEP!

S S S S S S S S S

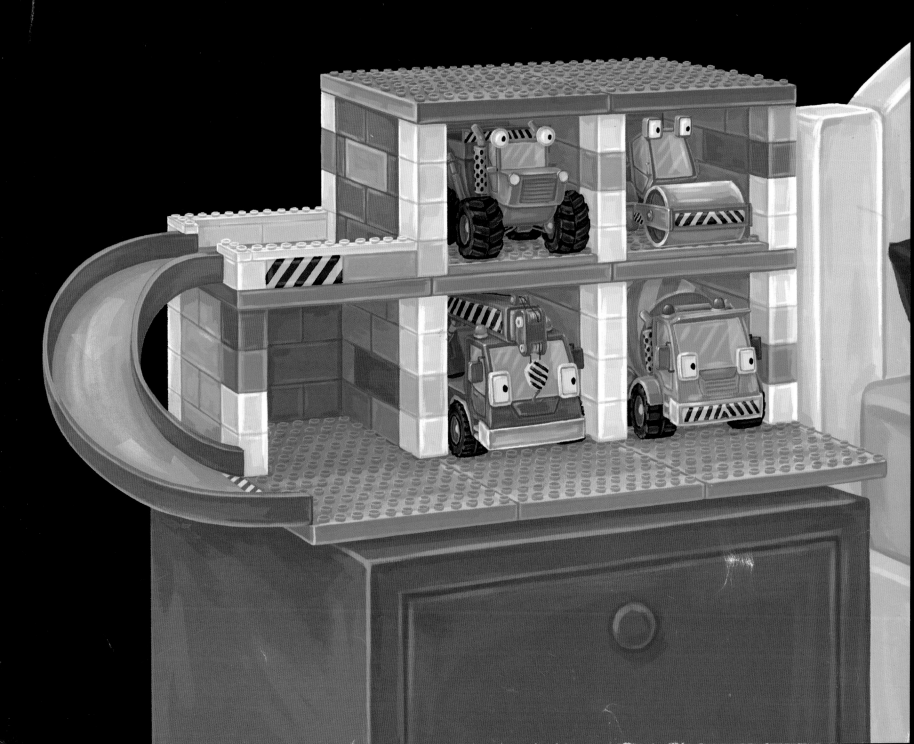

h h h h h h h h h h h h h h h h h h h